CATS

and the People They Own

CATS
and the People They Own

Ed Strnad
writing as
Lillian Lidofsky

Developed by The Philip Lief Group, Inc.

A Perigee Book

A Perigee Book
Published by The Berkley Publishing Group
200 Madison Avenue
New York, NY 10016

Published by arrangement with The Philip Lief Group, Inc.
6 West 20th Street
New York, NY 10011

First edition: April 1995

Published simultaneously in Canada.

Library of Congress Cataloging-in-Publication Data
Lidofsky, Lillian
    Cats and the people they own / Ed Strnad writing as Lillian
Lidofsky. — 1st ed.
        p.   cm.
    "Developed by the Philip Lief Group."
    "A Perigee book."
    ISBN 0-399-51908-4 (pbk. : alk. paper)
    1. Cats—Humor.   I. Title.
PN6231.C23L53   1995
818' .5402—dc20   94-5388
                                                   CIP

Printed in the United States of America.

10   9   8   7   6   5   4   3   2   1

This book is printed on acid-free paper.

Acknowledgments

*T*he author cattily acknowledges JoAnn Strnad, spouse; Lidia IIasenaucr, sister in-law; Judy Huson and Sheila Clemens, friends; Gary Sunshine, editor; and Stinky & Casper the Cats, owners.

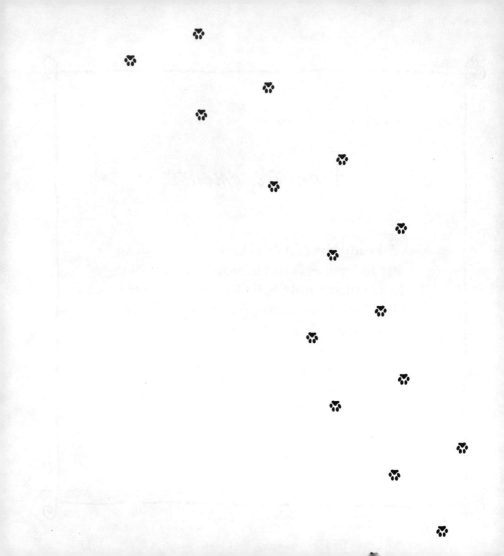

Introduction

*H*ave you ever dropped by a friend's house and noticed that her cat just seems to own the place? Everything's branded with scratch marks; the floor is littered with toys, and you have to schlep over a $49.95 deluxe model covered litter box to get to the john. Then just as you're about to park yourself, your hostess starts waving her hands frantically and says, "Do you mind sitting over here? That's Fuzzy's chair."

It's not like the cat's chipping in for the rent or anything. Let alone doing his share of the chores.

"Oh, but the *companionship*," your friend simpers. "The love and affection! The occasional smoked salmon, the occasional replacement lamp, the occasional reupholstering bill—it's a small price to pay!"

Frankly, my definition of a loving companion isn't someone who stays under the bed for hours at a stretch. Or for that matter, inside a paper bag, behind the curio cabinet, or on top of the refrigerator. I got more attention from my second husband, Sidney, and he wasn't any Mr. Romance, let me tell you.

Oh, little Fuzzy shows his face *once* in a while. He wouldn't want my friend to have to read the newspaper alone, for instance. Or go to sleep on a hot summer night without something warm and cozy covering her face. Of course, he's always glad to join in on her dinner parties, and he'll even be extremely careful not to land directly on the FiestaWare. Not that he could care less—he just doesn't want to get his little *feet* dirty.

Take it from me, these cat people are nuts. The cats maybe aren't so nuts. They've got a nice little racket going for themselves. Nap eighteen hours a day and wake up to a full bowl and a cooing, worshipful servant who wants nothing more than to stroke their fur coat and kiss their nose. Life's just a big catered affair.

Don't you see? Cats couldn't care less, so go ahead—*you* cough up a hairball and see what happens. You think he'll rush over to clean it up and say, "Ooh, poor baby?" He'll probably just sneer in disgust and go to another room. Can you see cats slaving eight hours a day, gazing across their desks at framed photos of the humans who are back home snoozing? Can you see them hanging up calendars full of glossy shots of the Human of the Month? Buying little paperback books to try and figure out human psychology?

Fat chance. They think they know better. That's why I've written this little list. Just to let them know they're not putting anything over on *me*. Just to set the record straight about what's really going on here. And just to make a little extra money. I need a new lamp, and what they're charging for smoked salmon at the deli now, I don't even want to tell you.

—*Lillian Lidofsky*

Note from Ed Strnad: This book has been written under the pseudonym "Lillian Lidofsky" in order to protect the innocent—namely, myself. My humorless kitties bristle at the slightest criticism; knowing them, they would probably call this book an act of supreme betrayal. To escape permanent damage to drapes, chairs, and plants, and to maintain harmony in my home, I'll let good old Ms. Lidofsky take the blame for the following labor of love.

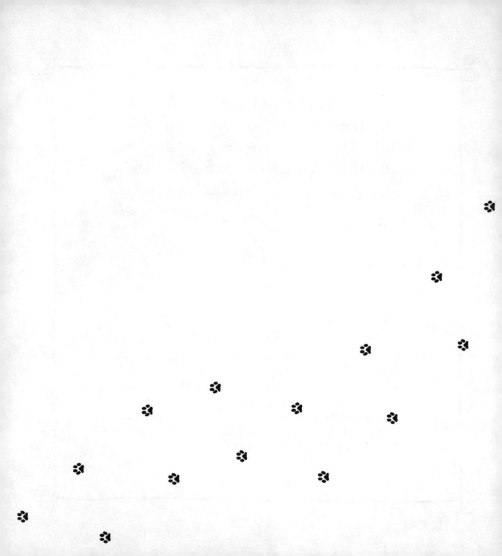

CATS

and the
People They
Own

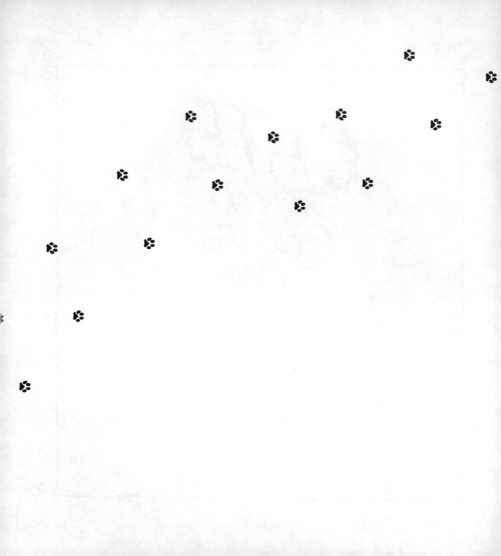

giving a sixteen-year-old cat a $20,000
kidney transplant

people who collect cat hair, spin it into
yarn, and weave it

considering cats intelligent when they
have brains the size of walnuts

discovering a whisker in your Caesar
salad, then discovering that the anchovies
have disappeared

the deeply disturbed offspring of
inbred cats

when the scratches on your arms are mis-
taken for the track marks of a drug addict

that the domestic cat has lived with
humans for more than 5,000 years but
still doesn't understand the word *No*

when kitty makes an appetizer out of your
expensive exotic bird

stockyard-strength odors wafting from the
litter box

clawed stereo speakers

 2

trying to get them to swallow hairball
medicine

how they eat all around a pill hidden in
their food

taking their temperature rectally

felines with diarrhea

canned cat food made of fetid fish guts

the smell of cat food after it's been sitting
in the bowl untouched for eight hours

finickiness

cats that will eat only room-temperature
food

cats that refuse to eat premium cat food,
but love to get into the garbage

people who feed their cats pâté

when watching your cat give birth gives
new meaning to the word *icky*

when a litter is delivered on your bed

that the average American cat consumes
more resources than the average Third
World person

fat cats with attitude

ninety-dollar vet visits

when tabby's annual medical bills
are bigger than yours

when they stare while you're eating,
telepathically beaming "Give me some"
thoughts at you

when they nonchalantly walk on the table
while you're eating

"gourmet" cat foods

permanently psycho Persians

traveling on an airplane with your cat

owning a white cat and a black wardrobe

endlessly picking cat hairs off your clothes

unaltered males that spray on everything
in sight, indoors and out

 6

mutant cats with six or more toes on
each paw

being in a small, airless bathroom
containing a litter box

going to the bathroom when the
cat is using its box

cats that have conniptions when hit by
a drop of water

cats that take up too much room on
your bed

cats that like to sleep on your head

inhaling more dander than air

tuna breath

when you have to make the bed over
your lazy cat, leaving a lump under
the covers

being allergic to cats

any cat named *Mister* something
(e.g., Mr. Sniffles)

 8

cats named after Egyptians (e.g., Nefertiti)

being ignored when you summon a cat
by name

when the cat likes to lie on the
most-trafficked stairway in your house

tripping over a cat

having your friendly advances rejected
by a haughty Siamese

how easy it is to run them ragged chasing
the spot from a flashlight

how no floor rug can remain flat for long
in a home containing a cat

"scaredy-cats" who spend their entire
lives hiding

sometimes suspecting they're really space
aliens wearing cat suits

when cats stare into their empty bowls
after eating, as if there still may be
subatomic food particles they missed

getting a shock from petting a cat on a
cold, dry day

when a cat has a "bad fur day"

sulkers

when they stalk your shoelaces

when firefighters waste valuable time
rescuing cats "stuck" in trees

not understanding what their meows
mean, except the "You're stepping on my
tail, moron!" sound

trying to give your cat a bath

using a blow-dryer on a cat

the excruciating sting of iodine on
cat scratches

cleaning scummy fur out of your tub

cats that eat weird food, like donuts

when you're watching a horror movie and
the cat pounces on you during the scariest
moment

kittens with needle-sharp claws tena-
ciously crawling up your legs

smelly dried spit caked in their fur

annual news stories about cats loose in a
jumbo-jet's cargo hold

cats having a sleep-to-wakefulness ratio of
greater than ten-to-one

when they spit up something in the middle of the night in the exact spot where
you'll step when you get out of bed

cats whose main expression is a contemp-
tuous sneer

calling them "domestic" animals when
they never cook or clean

when they stop licking suddenly and
look up, their tongues still sticking
halfway out

canned food that all looks and smells the
same, but bears different names, like
"Kitty Stew" and "Bits o' Beef"

magazines devoted to felines

tedious Broadway musicals about them

when they sniff something and their jaws
drop open in disgust

when Penelope spends hours trying to
shake a little water out of her paw

when old cats become un-housebroken

cat cemeteries

being licked raw by a rough tongue

when they go into a petting frenzy and
won't leave you alone

wondering if you're the only one who
finds Garfield more than a little *obnoxious*

when kitty's breath smells like
old gym socks

trying to brush your cat's teeth

trying to floss your cat's teeth

running out of iodine and Band-Aids
before kitty's teeth are clean

realizing that "meow" is composed
of "me" and "ow"

the twenty-five hideous diseases
transmitted by cats, like cat-scratch fever
and toxoplasmosis

litter-box mishaps that rival the *Exxon
Valdez* oil spill in toxicity

when your cat starts kicking turds out
of the box

wondering why your dog thinks cat turds
are tempting taste-treats

reading sickeningly sweet stories about
cats in *Reader's Digest*

moronic poetry about cats

getting a big kiss from kitty after she's
just licked her butt

when tabby gets too tubby

wasting money buying "diet" cat food

when your cat sucks in his cheeks to make
you think he's underfed and starving

when cats eat dog food

when your turtle mysteriously disappears

a cat loitering around your birdbath

when kitty drags a bird into the house and
there's blood and feathers everywhere

when kitty regurgitates partially digested
parts of some creature onto the rug

indelible barf stains in your carpets

when your pussy's too dumb to figure out
how to use a cat door

when they bite your toes through the
bed's blankets

trying to get them to pose for photographs

cats that always have those red "devil cat" eyes in photos

the months it takes a cat to readjust her internal clock to daylight saving time

when your cat turns off the alarm clock the morning of an important appointment

when they step on the remote control and change channels

when they start pestering you to feed
them an hour before mealtime

when they make a clumsy move or fall,
then act as if they meant to do it

cats wearing bows in their hair

when how fast the cat races out of the box
indicates how bad the smell is going to get

claws that never retract completely

the hassle of bringing another cat or dog
into your household

those bogus "Train Your Cat to Use the Toilet" products

pug-nosed cats who are ugly in a cute sort of way

binge eaters

when kitty projectile-hurls a hairball

cats that eat grass so that their spit-up will be topped with a decorative green garnish

when they go barreling past you down a flight of stairs

that cats never feel guilt for destroying
things

when the cat breaks something and tries
to make it look like the dog did it

when cats stupidly chase their own tails

cats addicted to catnip

that tennis rackets aren't really strung
with catgut

when they ricochet from sofa to chair
and back again

discovering that when they rub up
against you "affectionately," they're
actually marking you with secretions
from their scent glands

when a black cat crosses your path

when your wooden chair and table legs
get gnawed on

frayed and torn cushions on all your
couches, chairs, etc.

visitor-unfriendly cats

lies you tell your guests, like "She doesn't
scratch"

cats in heat who love to sleep on the
guest bed

noisy and violent turf battles with your dog

that to err is human, to never forgive feline

buying a cardboard cutout kitty and
receiving virtually the same amount of
love and affection as from the real thing

when they sneeze kitty snot on you

stories about a cat that somehow finds
its way home years after wandering to
another continent

when your cat gets lost going next door

listening to someone's long, boring story
about a cat they used to have

that they can't earn their keep by
becoming seeing-eye cats

that you can't send your cat to obedience
school

that if a burglar ever broke into your
house, your cat would roll over belly-up
in front of him

when they fillet your priceless oriental rug

enigmatic looks on their faces that
actually mean "When are you going to
feed me, bozo?"

when fat cats lie on your chest and con-
strict your breathing

wasting money on an expensive miniature
brass bed that Princess will never sleep in

when your cat is better groomed and
nourished than you are

electronic flea collars

driving with a cat loose in the car

when they throw up in your car on
the way to the vet

cats that sound exactly like
crying babies

show-biz cats that do tricks
on command

when your cat's only trick is sticking out
her tongue when you vigorously scratch
her rump

when your cat cries for food whenever
you open *any* can with the electric
can opener

one-eyed "pirate" cats

realizing that "independent" is cat-
language for "we hate people"

that no one will buy a previously
owned cat

getting spritzed with cat-food juice whenever you pop off the top of a can of food

the disgusting food-encrusted spoon you
use to feed the cat

cats that cause you to utter "damn it"
more than once a day

people who sing "What's New, Pussycat?"
to their pet

having the litter spill on the floor when
emptying the box

when combing their fur causes fleas to
hop onto your arm

"stealth" cats that come out of nowhere,
attack your ankle, then vanish

people who turn into mush at the sight
of a basket full of kittens

trying to give away your cat's litter
of kittens

when a stray cat decides to adopt *you*

a tablecloth matted with cat hair

dropping your toothbrush in the
litter box

emptying the litter box first thing in
the morning

finding hairs in your coffee cup

the movie *That Darned Cat*

swerving to avoid hitting a stray darting in
front of your car

when kitty knocks a flowerpot off the
windowsill to the sidewalk below

when your 100 percent cashmere sweater
becomes 10 percent cat hair

finding your cat stuck upside down on
your screen door

having to listen to a friend's anecdotes
about how clever (amazing, smart, etc.)
her cat is

a ten-year-old cat whose only special
talent is to come at the sound of a can
being opened

being your cat's door-opener

having to decide who keeps the cat when
you break up

year-round flea infestations in your
apartment

when a cat attacks your stuffed-animal
collection

when tabby scarfs down all the caviar at
your party

when kitty makes spooky scratchy sounds
on the front door at 3 A.M.

❖ 34 ❖

cats that scream "Feed me" the second you get out of bed

when your significant other's cat takes an active dislike to you

cats that greet you at the door only if it's feeding time

when your cat comes in with a wriggling praying mantis sticking halfway out of her mouth

when she places a gift of a dead rodent at your feet

caged birds driven neurotic by cats

finding buried treasures in your kid's
sandbox

living with a cat person when you're
a dog person

having to resort to rubbing fish oil on your
cheek to get a cat to kiss you

understanding why the Bible mentions
dogs eighteen times but never cats

cookbooks for cats

when people whose house stinks,
furniture is shredded, and clothes are
permanently fuzzy ask, "So why don't
you get a cat?"

when they knock your phone off the hook

when they walk across your face to wake
you up

cats that can eat continuously without
coming up for air

owning a cat so sickly that the vet's num-
ber is on your speed dialer

pee damage to your family heirloom
wedding dress

getting more hairball medicine on
yourself than in the cat

"cats rule and dogs drool" T-shirts

"I love my [cat breed]" bumper stickers

wishing their vaunted independence
would include opening doors and cans of
food by themselves

when the fur flies in a late-night cat fight

laid-back cats that burn up less than one
calorie an hour but crave tons of food

Hello Kitty merchandise

buying your cat a $200 kitty condo that
he rips to shreds in a week

cleaning up cat toenails from around the
scratching post

when the scratching post stays in pristine
condition but your upholstery doesn't

psychologists for cats

litter boxes that are designed to contain
odors but fail miserably

poopy old cats who don't clean themselves
as often as they used to

owners with cat co-dependency

that you could never get eight cats to team
up and pull a sled through snow

that no favor can win their gratitude

the fact that outdoor cats kill ten to fifty
birds a year

when your cat's back arches and tail puffs
up for no apparent reason

when the cat walks across your computer
keyboard

that if looks could kill, your cat would be
on death row

one word: *aloofness*

sneaky pussies that crawl around
crouched down on their bellies

strays that slink around your neighborhood

❖ 41 ❖

calendars with pictures of cats dressed up
and posed like people

cats having stained, grungy teeth
and matching foul breath

paying one hundred bucks annually to
have your cat's teeth cleaned

"My Cat Wishes Your Cat a Merry
Christmas" greeting cards

when cats remain interested in the
opposite sex even after being fixed

the cost of boarding a cat

the cost of spaying a queen

horny tomcats caterwauling outside all
night when your cat's in heat

when your purebred gets impregnated by
the neighborhood alley cat

people who are against spaying and
neutering

that cat burglars rarely steal felines

having to check every drawer for something
moving inside before shutting it

finding cat hair on your underwear

being unamused by their "adorable" antics

catnaps that last nine or ten hours, and
always during the daytime

pampered pussycats that have tasted
feathers only from a hat their owners
used to wear

when kitty bats around a ball of tinfoil in
the bathtub at 2 A.M.

trying to clip your cat's claws

when a stray cat gives birth under
your house

the thought of being reincarnated as a cat

the idea that you might have been a cat
in a past life

cats that refuse to eat cold chicken giblets

discovering that expensive breeds get
killed off quickly, but "mutt" cats are
indestructible

timid cats with mouseophobia

🐾 45 🐾

when you point to something you want
them to look at and they sniff your finger

when they drool on your lap while
being petted

trying to hold down your cat while
shaking flea powder on her

when flea powder turns up on everything

that the only sweet cat is made of
milk chocolate

exotic breeds that require special diets

when they're still shedding their winter
coats in July

not knowing how to determine the gender
of a kitten

that Captain Picard allows cats aboard
the *Enterprise*

how your cat gives you a third-degree
sniffing after you've been fooling around
with another cat

cats wearing jewel-studded collars worth
more than your car

the hunger strike they'll go on if you try to
switch them from canned food to dry

how their loyalty easily transfers from
their longtime owner to the very next
person holding a can of food

being ailurophobic

cats that don't purr

that all kittens eventually become cats

people who have cats pictured on their
personal checks

their half-closed eyes of contempt for you

being totally ignored by your kitty

that their claws unsheathe whenever they
sit on your lap

never having a pair of run-free stockings,
thanks to you-know-who

how peeved they get when you move them
in order to sit down

having to fish out toys from the litter box

having to be your cat's foster parent

cats that think they're human

the ability of your cuddly pet to suddenly
turn into a ferocious wild animal

their roles in pagan and occult rituals

when you want to watch a basketball game
on TV but your cat's in the way trying to
swat the ball

that they never want to go for "walkies"
with you

"magnetic" cats that seem to attract steel-
belted radials

when your cat's Christmas stocking is bigger than yours

when you roll over in bed onto your cat
and he snarls and bites you

wiping blood off your face after kitty races
over the bed and your head

when he watches you take a shower

when you start singing in the shower
and he leaves in disgust

the cat's ability to stare for hours without
blinking

when they bite and pull your hair

when they walk across the piano keys

cats that follow you obsessively

French books for cats

that "stay" and "come" are foreign words
as far as your cat is concerned

when kitty knocks over your chess pieces

wool-sweater munchers

that the I.R.S. won't let you claim
your cats as dependents on your
tax returns

picking up a hairball with your
bare hands

that fetching is beneath them

how they always seem to know when
you're talking about them

when your kitty takes an ultra-stinky
dump

when they turn their heads and just
glare at you

that by the time you finish this sentence,
one hundred more cats will have been born

clipping a claw too close to the quick

treating claw-clipping injuries

when you inherit your ex-roommate's cat

being intimidated by their self-reliance

when they lick your nose to get your attention while you're trying to read

when you've vacuumed up enough bird feathers to go into the pillow business

muddy paw prints that clash with the pattern on your carpet

cats that wouldn't bat an eyelash if you got mugged in front of them

when the stray that hangs around
your house has you wrapped around
her little paw

when the "stray" turns out to be your
neighbor's cat, looking for a handout

when your cat knocks over a wastebasket
and pulls the trash out of it

cats that do something nasty to spite you
for going away and leaving them alone

when they cry constantly to be picked up,
yet hate to be held

when your "little stinker" passes gas
when you pick him up

when the cat fights for your drinking
straw before you're done with it

felines that lose all their toys under the
stove and refrigerator

when they steal and hide little
 things, like your diamond ring or
contact lens case

how they lie on top of the clothes you've
laid out whenever possible

when the cat laps milk from your glass
when you're not looking

lifting a thirty-pound bag of kitty litter

when they get jealous if you talk on the
phone, watch a video, or sit at a PC

when you want to lavish attention on
them and they want you to bug off

when they noisily clean their private parts
while company is visiting

deaf albino cats

when your lover objects to sleeping in a
bed with more than one species at a time

when a cat with worms drags his butt
across the floor

when they scratch up your couch while
defiantly looking straight at you

trying to walk them on a leash

that a cat doesn't wag its tail when
it is happy

when kitty unrolls all the toilet paper

when one of your cats won't use the box
because another cat has, and goes on the
floor next to the box instead

that a sweet little cat could be a witch's
familiar

cats that never warn you of impending
earthquakes

oddball cats that seem to be afflicted with
some form of brain damage

when your cats' only interests in life are
eating and sleeping

people who say your cat takes after you,
eating-wise and sleeping-wise

when your sleeping cat suddenly shoots
straight up into the air

cats that never do anything interesting
when you videotape them

people who buy videos of swimming fish
to entertain their cats

that no matter how hard you try, you can't
teach them to catch a Frisbee

having cat-nose prints on your windows

paw prints across your car's hood, roof, and trunk

when your cat brings home a flopping fish from a local pond

mistaking a wild feral cat for a pettably cute kitten

smug city cats

coastal cats that regard the beach as one gigantic litter box

seeing the same flattened cat in the road
for weeks on your way to work

the toxic smell of flea and tick collars

when cats eat defenseless baby birds

when kitty chews up your favorite plants

when she'd rather play with your toys
than her toys

that cats don't have to be licensed

unimaginative names for cats, like "Felix"

❖   63   ❖

when kitty's summertime diet consists
mainly of bugs

owners who claim their cats understand
spoken words

when your cat jumps up on the bed
during an intimate moment

wishing you could fill your cat's box
with quicksand

people who scorn you for declawing
your cat

when cats regurgitate in front of company

that disgusting goop that oozes from
cats' eyes

when they sniff something on the
ground, like a dead fish, then collapse
and roll around on it

faster-than-a-speeding-bullet cats

when tabby runs roughshod over
everything in his path—including you

when their ears get infested with mites

putting drops of oil in their ears

when they shake their heads, flinging
the oil all over you

having to put an Elizabethan collar on
them to stop ear scratching

cats who fall twenty stories and live

when your cat's a fly-catcher *and*
a lip-kisser

when they sit and stare at nothing for
hours

when you finally get the cat to swallow her
pill and she spits it up

when they'd rather play with a tinfoil ball
than an expensive toy

trying to get your cat into the cat carrier

having to shake the carrier to dislodge the
cat inside

moving your couch and discovering
dozens of lost cat toys

having to pretend you like your lover's cat

cats that like to chew buttons off your
shirts, dresses, etc.

phone-cord tanglers

when your rich aunt dies and leaves her
entire estate to her cats

"hood ornament" kitties that sleep on
your car

when kitty finds out that cats and auto
engines don't mix

when they climb your Christmas tree

the old wives' tale about cats stealing
babies' breath

cat-sex noise outside that keeps
you awake

their ability to leap high enough to reach
any shelf, ledge, counter, etc.

when kitty's tail accidentally slips under
a rocking chair

when they shred your fancy flocked
wallpaper

living next door to a weirdo who owns
132 cats

a cat's terror upon having its head held
out a car window

cats that won't let anyone hug them

cats that bite the hand that feeds them

when kitty nibbles at your mounted fish
trophy

fat dormant cats that could do double
duty as doorstops

having to hear dumb jokes every time
someone sees your tailless Manx

breeds that shed in the winter, spring,
summer, and fall

out-of-control biting and scratching

cats that should carry a warning label:
"Hazardous When Wet"

catching your cat's cold

realizing that your cat doesn't give a damn
if you live or die

cat palindromes, such as "Was it a car, or
a cat I saw?"

wondering why Morris the Cat is famous
when every cat is just as finicky

owners who kiss their cats on the mouth

people who carry a wallet full of pictures
of their cats

owners who get their cat's portrait
done in oils

"Beware of Attack Cat" signs

having to hide your kitty from your
"no pets" landlord

trying to get your cat to wear a cute
little hat

when a Chia Pet is more affectionate than
your cat

an album of Christmas songs "sung" by
mewing cats

when your cat decimates your collection
of expensive tropical fish

their uncanny ability to amuse themselves
at your expense

when kitty uses your favorite plant as a
convenient litter box

cats that snore

hearing your spouse and cat snoring
in stereo

when your baby's first word is the
cat's name

cat owners who treat their pets like children

parents who treat their cats better than
their children

having to send your flabby tabby to a
"fat farm"

when your pussy's too wussy to kill a
humongous spider in your bathroom

coming home to a cat who's not happy to
see you

when people risk their lives to rescue a cat
from a burning building

that no movie or TV cat was ever as
famous as Lassie

when the cat makes off with your
lobster tail

when a pedigreed cat has five official
names, but everyone just calls it "Max"

having to rescue your cat stranded
in deep snow

that a "clowder of cats" sounds so much
classier than a "pack of dogs"

when your cat wants to smell your breath
after you've eaten sardines

petting a cat whose fur comes out
in clumps

that they never wipe their paws before
coming indoors

that Socks, the First Cat, has yet to write a
best-selling book

cats that cry to be let out, then immediately
wail to be let back in

skittish felines that hiss at their reflections
in the mirror

condominiums that fine you if you let
your cat out without a leash

having your twitching toes ambushed
when you're fast asleep

"cat-tastrophies," like when Tigger knocks
over your Tiffany lamp

books on how to give your cat a massage

the cost of all-natural, low-ash cat food

wishing your kitty would give you a
clawless massage just once

owners who claim that their cat thinks
he's a dog

buying bottles of nontoxic flea shampoo
that cost more than any designer product
you've ever owned

suspecting that your cat loves its food dish
more than you

cats that wake up in a manic mood

when kitty anoints your bed pillow
with some brackish bodily fluid as
a sign of affection

being a sucker for a plaintive meow

when your cat knows you're a soft touch

when the neighbor's cat drives your cat nuts
by peering into your living room window

that your cat's mysterious expression
could mean she's contemplating the
meaning of life, or just wondering what's
for din-din

hyperactive cats that are always bouncing off the walls

when kitty incessantly chases a fly all over the house, breaking multiple bric-a-brac in the process

when he glowers at you for hours because you accidentally stepped on his tail

when you treat your cat like a human, and she treats you like a dog

when your cat has a psychotic reaction at the sight of a vacuum cleaner

worrying in the morning when your cat
didn't come home last night

when she comes home, sprayed by a skunk

cats that will play with a ball of foil until
they drop from exhaustion

anticipating the claws when they knead
your belly and other tender parts of
your anatomy

discovering revolting little creepy-crawlies
in your cat's coat

when they heartlessly insist on their
6 A.M. feeding, even on weekends

when Snowball has a nightmare and her
twitching feet awaken you

Art Spiegelman's "Maus" cartoons, in
which Nazis are portrayed as cats

the saying, "There's more than one way
to skin a cat"

granules of litter tracked all over your
apartment

when people imply that men who own
cats are somehow un-macho

the delightful task of sifting the chunks
out of "reusable" litter

when the neighbors complain that your
cat beat up their cat

when the neighbors complain that your
cat beat up their dog

acrobatic "circus cats" who can do
a double-flip with a half-twist onto
your back

when your little "Fluffy" loves to go out
and brawl every night

the subversive power that the act of
holding a purring kitten has to convert
you into a cat owner

not realizing that you're getting into a
twenty-year commitment when you
accept that ball of fluff

finding out firsthand why the cat you
adopted was named "Fireball"

that NASA never shot a cat up into space

felines that like to bat at dangling earrings

people who consider cats New Age pets

tallying up the cost of cat ownership and
being unpleasantly surprised

when your cat slams into the window
trying to catch the bird on the
other side

calicoes gone loco on catnip

waking up to see a cat's butt two inches
away from your face

when they lick your eyelids first thing in
the morning

hearing a hiss, a growl, and a crash coming
from the next room

having to go out in a snowstorm because
you're out of litter

the homeless cats in every city

books about cats that outsell
Hemingway's novels

Life magazine photo-features of sleeping cats

owners who speak baby talk to their cats

when your cat's color clashes with your
home's decorating scheme

Keane's paintings of pathetic big-eyed kittens and kids

the "great hunters" who never take care of
the bugs in your bedroom

whimsical kitty calendars

when your fat cat falls over and the record
player skips

wondering what a "cat's cradle" has to do
with felines

mixed breed, random-bred, and other
euphemisms for "mutt cat"

brats who toss cats into swimming pools

when their mewing wakes up the baby

Tom from *Tom and Jerry*

failing to get your cat to meow to
someone over the phone

knowing your cat is listening because even
though his back is to you, his ears are
turned in your direction

when your cat's cutest stance is her attack
position

declawed toms who still think they
have claws, but are rudely reminded
when leaping up a tree trunk

having to read *The Cat in the Hat* five times
a day to your kid

cats that look at you cross-eyed

when kitty plays with your pen while
you're trying to write

people who make invidious comparisons
between feline behavior and female
behavior

owners decked out in cat paraphernalia,
such as cat earrings, T-shirts, rings, etc.

cats that have whiskers sprouting from
just one side of their faces

the thought that the afterlife might be
populated by cats

when Fluffy claws your water bed and
punctures it

having to buy a training doll to help your
cat adjust to your newborn

when the refrigerator door closes on the
cat's tail

flaky cats who have dandruff

wondering if the stray that's just nipped
you has had all her shots

getting the evil eye from a black cat

having to stop to feed your cats when
you're late for work

when a mommy cat bites, kicks, and
abuses her kittens

when your neighbor lets his cat outside so
it can crap on your lawn

when spayed or neutered cats lose their
personality

how your tomcat never forgives you for
getting him fixed

exercise equipment for cats

understanding why being called "catty" is
not a compliment

ceramic cat collections

being your cat's "person"

wondering what your cat's pet name for
you would be

when the cats in the pet store are asleep

having to bell a bird-catching cat

dumb birds that aren't scared by the
sound of a bell

wanting to wash your hands after petting a
cat with a greasy coat

the pathetic pictures of cats on cans and
boxes of cat food

being kept awake by your cat's sucky-
sounds as she gets ready to go to sleep

having six different brands of cat litter to
choose from in the supermarket

when your kitty loses her friskiness

cats that can't be bothered to play
with yarn

the annoying *ack-ack* sound cats make
when they see a bird through a window

when they spend hours a day licking
their genitals

when cats begin to take over your life

when your cat tries to eat a Tootsie Roll
and it gets stuck on her teeth

when kitty sadistically torments a moth
all day without killing it

being snowbound with cabin-fevered cats

apartment-dwelling cats that are always
trying to get outside

having to shave your mangy cat

when the neighbors make fun of your
"hairless" cat

cat breeds you don't know how to
pronounce correctly, like "Abyssinian"

stepping on a squeaky toy in the middle
of the night and scaring yourself

throwing your money away on an
expensive wicker cat bed

stumbling to the bathroom in the dark
and stepping barefoot into the litter box

noticing too late that you're petting a cat
with a nasty skin disorder

when her look of deep thought really
means "My belly itches, but I'm too tired
to lick it"

when someone names her cat after you

that you can't teach an old cat new tricks
(or young ones either)

Tweety-Bird mimics who say, "I tought I
taw a Puddy-tat"

when you cook your cat a nice meal and
she just walks away from it

that a cat will never bite someone you
don't like on command

when Velcro sticks to your cat

🐾 99 🐾

the statistic that the average cat owner will
spend 802 hours in a lifetime emptying
the litter box

the statistic that there are over thirty
million overweight cats

when your cat takes over the empty
half of the bed whenever your spouse
is away

owners who throw lavish birthday parties
for their cats

people who wrap the gifts they give to cats

couples who get cats in lieu of having kids

when your mate tells you what the cat did today when you come home from work

dressing your cat in a Santa suit and calling him "Sandy Claws"

receiving a Christmas card with a picture of the sender's cat on it

cat-showing competitions

stressed-out cats that over-groom themselves to death

that moment when their eyes grow really
big and you know a bite is coming

magazine articles on celebrities' cats

Sylvester the cartoon cat's spitty lisp

when you hear on the news that cat fleas
carry the bubonic plague

the pangs of guilt and anxiety you feel
when you come home late and realize
kitty hasn't been fed

drooly Cheshire cat grins

when they use the scratching post only
when you're watching

not having the stomach to face that
glop called cat food so early in the
morning

when Catwoman licks Batman's face in
Batman Returns

when kitty steals your makeup brush

the irresistible compulsion they have to
climb into every box they see

when they open the cupboard and sit on
the dishes inside

when kitty wants to assist you in putting
in your contact lenses

cats that flinch whenever you reach to pat
their heads

when all your house plants downwind of
the litter box die

that cats mature sexually by three months
of age

that their 63-day gestation period means
they can have their first litter when only
five months old

having to give your kittens to the pound
because no one will adopt them

that cats don't appreciate the fact that
their lion and tiger relatives in the wild eat
only twice a week

when your cat closes her eyes while being
reprimanded

a wet slimy nose purring in your ear

cats that look nervous when you watch
them using their box

cats that come home soaked in
"Dumpster juice"

when you are your cat's chief source
of entertainment

having to rewind yards of yarn unraveled
all over the place

their resemblance to large skinny rats
when they're wet

aging cats that transform into amorphous
blobs with no distinguishing features
except their heads

when your klepto-kitty steals your
golf balls

their vastly overrated reputation
for cleanliness

when they sleep so long that you have to
check to see if they're still breathing

people who have photographs of their cats
on their desks at work

when people make "witty" remarks about your snub-nosed Persian like "Hey, who hit your cat in the face with a brick?"

owners who go orgasmic over every new issue of *Cat Fancy* magazine

cabinets containing boxes of old stale cat treats from the 1980s

tickling a cat's foot and discovering that cats really have no sense of humor

that you can't rent a cat before deciding to adopt it

people who swear that their cats smile

when kitty goes nuts whenever you open a
jar of pickled herring

cats named "Aerial" because they sleep on
top of the TV set

when your cat eats your Chia Pet

owners loyal to their cats, even though
their cats don't deserve it

cats that wear a look of superiority on
their pusses

realizing that if cats could talk, very few
people would own them

meeting a cat so ornery even Will Rogers
wouldn't have liked him

cat owners who have a soft spot in their
hearts and heads for their pets

when your cat keeps all the mice away,
and all the songbirds, too

when your "ex" is nicer to your cat than to you

horoscopes for cats

newborn kittens that look like hairy
meatballs

that you can't divorce your shrewish
silver longhair

owners who are amused by everything
their cats do—annoying, destructive,
or otherwise

getting your cat a tattooed I.D.

people who think that cats are good judges
of a person's character

being stuck with a basketful of scrappy
crappy kitties

the look you get from the rancid furball
when you sit in "the cat's chair"

when the cat insists on sitting in your spot
on the couch

that cats never develop sore throats or get
laryngitis after meowing all night

when your cat swallows a ribbon and you
have to watch for it to reappear

when your yawning kitty makes you
yawn, too

Felix the Cat's unctuous "Righty-Oh!"

blowing three bucks to rent the animated
Disney movie *The Aristocats*

that they don't show *Top Cat* cartoons on
TV anymore

friends and lovers who express tender
emotions to their cats that they never
express to you

owning a cat that resembles Charles
Manson

yuppies who own a pair of matching cats

wondering why something cool was once
referred to as "the cat's pajamas"

cats with dyed fur

when your cats commit incest

when they poison themselves from eating
butterflies, mistletoe, chocolate, etc.

discovering aspirin is poisonous to cats
after giving one to your sick tabby

cutting your finger on the edge of a can of
cat food

when your queen gets a reputation for
promiscuity

owners wearing sweatshirts emblazoned
with Kliban cat drawings

when you're walking down a dark alley
and a snarling cat scares the crap out
of you

when a kitten plays chicken with
a candle flame

the god-awful stench of singed cat fur

owners who enroll their cats in the Meal
of the Month Club

the fact that cats are not easily impressed

when your kitty comes home *after* you
post a hundred "lost cat" posters around
the neighborhood

smirky stud males

the odd fact that all calicoes are female

cats' overrated ability to see in the dark

that their slit-pupil eyes make them look
so ominous in Stephen King movies

pussy-footers that go *clickety-click* when
walking on linoleum

restaurants that have doggie bags, but no
"cat bags" for cat owners

that cats usually eat sitting down, while
dogs eat standing up

hippie bookstores that always have
cats in residence

when your cat's hygiene habits are a lot
like Stimpy's on *Ren & Stimpy*

that people who don't own cats can't
relate to any of this

owners who grow grass in a
cup for their cats' chewing and
regurgitating fun

when your cat pulls all the fur off her belly
with her teeth

knowing more than you ever wanted to
know about the workings of your cat's
urinary system

that you can get a miniature dog, but there
aren't any mini-cats

when your cat the critic pees on
Millie's Book

cats that don't know what to do with mice
once they catch them

discovering that at least 100 percent of all
cats are neurotic

watching a kitten waste its life chasing
some lint

that everything an owner needs to know
about cats fits in a very slim book

realizing that no matter how much cats
fight, there always seems to be plenty
of kittens

never having enough time to appreciate
your cat's timeless grace and beauty

when pregnant kitties sit up to beg and
topple over

the fact that cats are seldom kidnapped
because no one will pay more than ten
cents in ransom

cats whose best trick is playing dead

funerals for deceased felines

never seeing what some owners see in
their cats

unbalanced felines that don't always land
on their feet

owners who write love letters to cats

❧ 121 ❧

when your cat's a spoiled overfed
pampered pussy

when someone rudely refers to your
Japanese Bobtail as "Stumpy"

striped cats that could be used as a TV
test pattern

when your cats hear another cat on TV
and search the house looking for it

when your kitty watches over your
shoulder while you're working on a
crossword puzzle

when they check their bowls every hour
to see if something has been put in them

jaded cats with nothing better to do all day
than lie around, idly swatting flies

bored owners who spend all day
writing about their pets on computer
bulletin boards

when your cat is so fertile she could get
pregnant just by using a male's litter box

when you can't get rid of leftovers by
feeding them to your cats

when a cat scratch in childhood leads to
a lifelong aversion to the furry creatures

cats that run sideways

cats that can never get enough brushing
and combing

how when you move a couch, the cat
always curls up on the freshly exposed
clean patch of carpet

not having the freedom to just come and
go as you please

being beholden to another living thing

that cats can be happy and content leading
such dull, routine, and uneventful lives

that cats have been able to sucker humans
into providing for their every need

that humans don't seem to mind too
much

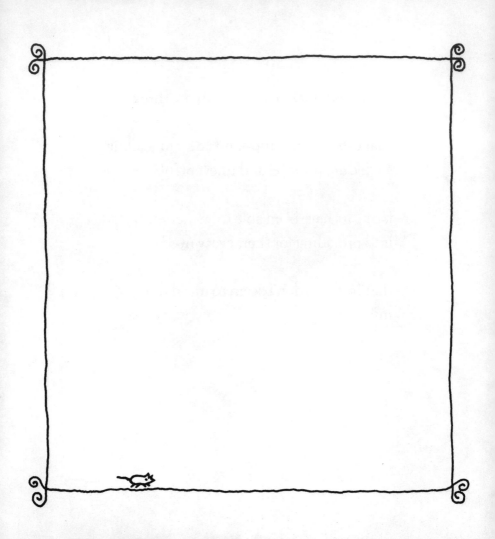